For all my friends, real and imagined. —A. V.

For Quinnie! Whee!! —H. C.

First published in the United States of America in June 2013
by Walker Books for Young Readers, an imprint of Bloomsbury Publishing, Inc.
www.bloomsbury.com

For information about permission to reproduce selections from this book, write to
Permissions, Walker BFYR, 175 Fifth Avenue, New York, New York 10010
Bloomsbury books may be purchased for business or promotional use. For information on bulk purchases
please contact Macmillan Corporate and Premium Sales Department at specialmarkets@macmillan.com

Library of Congress Cataloging-in-Publication Data
Vernick, Audrey.
Bogart and Vinnie : a completely made-up story of true friendship / Audrey Vernick, Henry Cole.
pages   cm
Summary: Vinnie, a "crazy-happy" dog, finds a most unlikely companion when visiting a nature preserve.
ISBN 978-0-8027-2822-7 (hardcover) · ISBN 978-0-8027-2823-4 (reinforced)
[1. Dogs—Fiction. 2. Rhinoceroses—Fiction. 3. Friendship—Fiction. 4. Wildlife refuges—Fiction.]
I. Cole, Henry, illustrator. II. Title.
PZ7.V5973Bo 2013   [E]—dc23   2012027335

Art created with acrylic paints, colored pencil, and ink on Arches hot press watercolor paper
Typeset in Hank Roman and Humana Sans Light
Book design by Nicole Gastonguay

Printed in China by C&C Offset Printing Co., Ltd., Shenzhen, Guangdong
1 3 5 7 9 10 8 6 4 2 (hardcover)
1 3 5 7 9 10 8 6 4 2 (reinforced)

All papers used by Bloomsbury Publishing, Inc., are natural, recyclable products
made from wood grown in well-managed forests. The manufacturing processes
conform to the environmental regulations of the country of origin.

Bogart and Vinnie

A Completely Made-Up
Story of True Friendship

AUDREY VERNICK   illustrated by HENRY COLE

WALKER BOOKS FOR YOUNG READERS
AN IMPRINT OF BLOOMSBURY
NEW YORK LONDON NEW DELHI SYDNEY

Hap was heading to work at Wildlands Preserve when he spotted Vinnie.

Lost animals can be dangerous.

He would need to proceed with caution.

Before Hap could catch the dog and bring him to the shelter, Vinnie took off.

Way in back, rarely visited, stood
Bogart, a square-lipped rhinoceros.

He breathed in the grassy peace of the
rhino range—his alone.

He cherished the quiet, his tail curled
with happiness.

Vinnie raced
straight toward Bogart
as though reuniting
with an old friend.

I love you!
I'm Vinnie!
Hi!

Nobody knew what attracted Vinnie to Bogart.
Was it his color? His shape? His horn? His other
horn? The way he completely ignored Vinnie?

Hap knew that rhinos could be dangerous. He had to lure Vinnie away.

He tried everything.

Nothing worked.

Hap needed a new plan.

Vinnie would not leave Bogart's side.

Nobody knew what attracted Bogart to Vinnie. Was it his bouncy energy? His crazy-happy tail? The fun games he played?

Bogart took off after Vinnie.

And that's how the two friends discovered their favorite game: Follow the Leader.

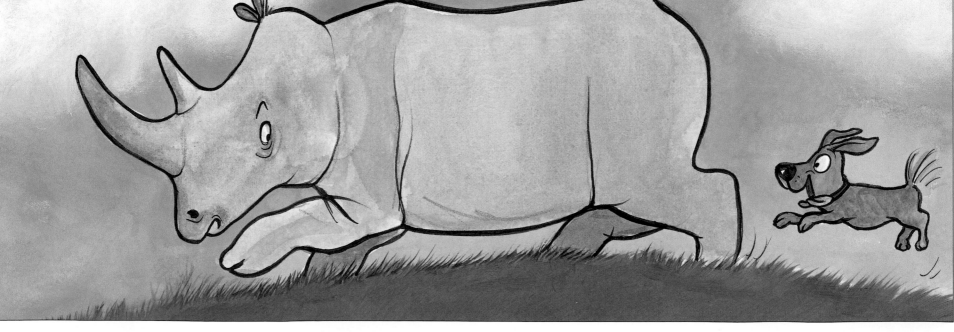

Meanwhile, Vinnie's owners were looking for him.

PINE ST

ELM ST

MISSING!

The boy, Ethan, worried that Vinnie was scared and alone.

Ethan couldn't have been more wrong!

I want to roll in this smell with you.

Nose friend! Smell this!

First me, then you.

Smell this best smell!

The friends played together all day. During Hide and Seek, Vinnie was always It!

No matter where Bogart hid, Vinnie found him.

Hap had never seen Bogart look so peaceful.

Overnight, Bogart and Vinnie became big news! The world was charmed by their unlikely friendship. Reporters flocked to Wildlands.

Polka and Dot showed off their stripes. The parrots cawed and chanted, "Hello! Look at parrots! Look at parrots!"

The reporters ignored them. Two zebras? Five parrots? So what?

Bogart and Vinnie had
an *interspecies* friendship.

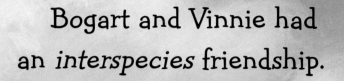

Suddenly, Bogart and Vinnie were famous! Their fans on the Internet watched everything they did.

There was no end to the fun they had together.

Vinnie's tail nearly wagged off from joy. Bogart's tail did not. It had lost its curl.

But their fame didn't last.

TIMES DISPATCH

JAVIER AND JENNA, SPIDER MONKEY AND HUMP-BACKED OX, BRAVE BLINDING BLIZZARD TO RESCUE STRANDED ORPHANS

SUN TRIBUNE

FELICITY, MONARCH BUTTERFLY, JOINS PACK OF LIONS, TEACHING GENTLER WAY OF LIFE

WEATHER

That was okay with Bogart and Vinnie. Because they had formed the kind of family where one member loves the other and one wants nothing more than to be left alone.

But, still, a family.

Vinnie's other family never gave up their search. But they were looking in all the wrong places! When they finally saw Bogart and Vinnie on the Internet, they raced to Wildlands.

Vinnie was extra crazy-happy to see them.

But no one could stand the thought of separating
the square-lipped rhinoceros and the crazy-happy dog.

Ethan's family decided to adopt Bogart.
(How much trouble could one rhino be?)
But, really, everyone at
Wildlands had been like
family to Vinnie. So
Ethan's family also took:

Polka and Dot,
the zebras,

the five *look-at-parrots* parrots,

and Hap, who, after all, had
rescued Vinnie.

They piled into the car.

What a heartwarming sight:
many species, living together
in peace and harmony.
Everyone was happy.

Except the neighbors.

UTAH
Past and Present

Jacqueline Ching

New York

For Scotia and Dagny

Published in 2011 by The Rosen Publishing Group, Inc.
29 East 21st Street, New York, NY 10010

Library of Congress Cataloging-in-Publication Data

Ching, Jacqueline.
Utah: past and present / Jacqueline Ching. — 1st ed.
    p. cm. — (The United States: past and present)
Includes bibliographical references and index.
ISBN 978-1-4358-9497-6 (library binding)
ISBN 978-1-4358-9524-9 (pbk)
ISBN 978-1-4358-9558-4 (6-pack)
1. Utah—Juvenile literature. I. Title.
F826.3.C47 2010
979.2—dc22

2010002493

Manufactured in Malaysia

CPSIA Compliance Information: Batch #S10YA: For further information, contact Rosen Publishing, New York, New York, at 1-800-237-9932.

On the cover: Top left: The Saltair Pavilion on the Great Salt Lake; it was destroyed by fire in 1925. Top right: The Salt Lake Temple in Temple Square, Salt Lake City. Bottom: A horseback riding excursion in Bryce Canyon.

Contents

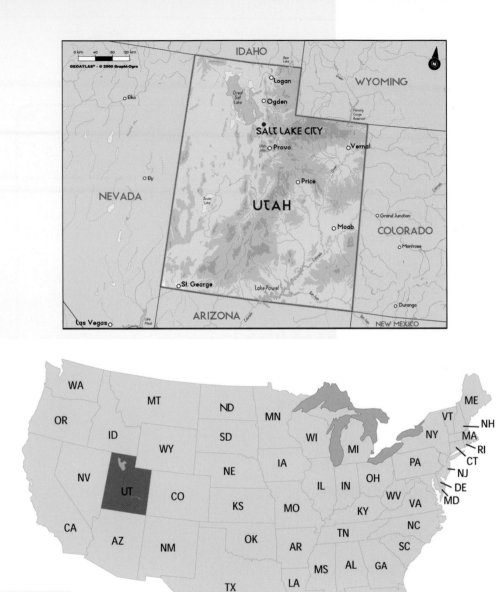

Utah is a western state bordered by Arizona on the south, New Mexico on the southeast, Colorado on the east, Wyoming on the northeast, Idaho on the north, and Nevada on the west. It was the forty-fifth state admitted to the Union. It is the thirteenth in area and the thirty-fourth in population.

Introduction

Utah's spectacular landscape is the ideal backdrop for the stories of human perseverance, devotion, and achievement that make up the state's history. The mountains, deserts, and red-rock canyons were the dramatic natural setting for the mysterious emergence and disappearance of the Anasazi and Fremont Native American cultures. They provided the harsh setting for the wild adventures of mountain men. Most famously, Utah's natural, awe-inspiring beauty was viewed as a new paradise. It was a majestic location that would become the stopping point and home of the Mormon Church, whose members had made the arduous journey from Illinois to escape persecution back east.

Grit, determination, and a relentless drive to keep pushing forward still characterize the people of Utah. They have created a flourishing culture and a sophisticated civilization in an often arid and infertile landscape. The state boasts several major cities, a robust economy, a vibrant cultural scene, a diverse population, academic excellence, and high-tech enterprises.

All of this productive and creative energy, striving for progress, and achievement continue to take place against one of the world's most stunning natural backdrops. From the Wasatch Mountains to the Great Salt Lake, from the gravity-defying sandstone formations of Arches National Park to the otherworldly and graceful red-rock hoodoo spires of Bryce Canyon, Utah is a place like no other in the world.

Chapter 1

THE GEOGRAPHY OF UTAH

Utah, a state in the western United States, is home to some of the country's most dramatic natural features. These include gleaming deserts and majestic mountains, and lush pine forests and marshes. The state's rivers and streams cut into layers of rock that hold fossils from all thirteen periods of the geologic time scale (only seven periods are shown in the Grand Canyon).

The state has three main geological regions: the Rocky Mountains, the Great Basin and Range, and the Colorado Plateau. The Rocky Mountains are found in northeastern Utah. The Uintah and Wasatch mountains are within this range. The Great Basin and Range is an area of deserts and mountain ranges that are separated by broad valleys. The Colorado Plateau lies in the east-central and southeastern parts of Utah. Colorful cliffs, arches, and other rock formations rise through this region. Wind and water formed them over millions of years. Rivers have carved canyons through the rock.

Climate

Utah's desert and mountainous terrain help give it very extreme annual temperatures—very cold winters and very hot summers. Average summertime temperatures can be as high as 100 degrees

The red sandstone buttes of Utah's Monument Valley shoot up hundreds of feet into the sky. For the early Native Americans who lived there, it was considered a supernatural place.

Fahrenheit (38 degrees Celsius), while winter lows often dip below 0°F (-18°C). Most of Utah has an arid or semiarid climate. While the mountains can receive 700 inches (1,778 centimeters) of snowfall per year and Salt Lake City receives about 60 inches (152 cm), lowland areas receive less than 12 inches (30 cm) of precipitation. Desert areas can see less than 3 inches (8 cm) per year.

Flora and Fauna

Utah is home to more than four thousand plant and animal species. Large mammals include mule deer, pronghorn antelope, Rocky

Lake Bonneville

The lakes of Utah have gone through many cycles over the last few millions of years. During the ice ages, when the climate of the region was cooler and wetter, water levels rose. A rise in water level about twenty-five thousand years ago produced Lake Bonneville. It was one of the largest prehistoric lakes that were once abundant in western Utah and Nevada. It was roughly the size of Lake Michigan. At its peak, it covered 19,691 square miles (51,000 square kilometers) and was 1,000 feet (305 meters) deep. Lake Bonneville stretched out over most of western Utah and parts of Idaho and Nevada. It was located in the Great Basin, which today is a large, arid region.

Early inhabitants were drawn to the Great Basin, where food was plentiful. At one time, Lake Bonneville contained fresh water. Big game like saber-toothed cats, mammoths, mastodons, and ground sloths, which grew up to 17 feet (5 m) and weighed as much as 5 tons (5,000 kilograms), once roamed there. Later, bison, antelope, and mule deer took their place. After the last ice age, temperatures rose, the lake dried up, and the area's salinity increased. Today, the lake is just a prehistoric memory, but its waters did leave some remnants: the Great Salt Lake, Little Salt Lake, Utah Lake, Sevier Lake, and Rush Lake. The Great Basin is a 200,000-square-mile (518,000 sq km) plateau that covers most of Nevada and more than half of Utah. It receives most of its precipitation from snow that melts in the spring. However, the rain that is produced evaporates quickly in the dry desert environment.

The largest remnants of Lake Bonneville are the Great Salt Lake, Utah Lake, Great Salt Lake Desert, and Sevier Lake. The Great Salt Lake and the Great Salt Lake Desert, which contains the Bonneville Salt Flats, are 4,000 square miles (10,360 sq km) of the flattest terrain in the world. Salt deposits 6 feet (2 m) deep have been measured in many areas of the Bonneville Salt Flats. Many movies have been filmed here, including *Pirates of the Caribbean 3: At World's End*.

Mountain bighorn sheep, lynx, grizzly and black bears, and white-tailed and black-tailed jackrabbits. The state is also home to more than five dozen species of snakes and lizards and more than seven dozen species of fish, including trout, bass, shad, perch, walleye, pike, catfish, whitefish, and bluegill.

Utah is a birder's paradise, with native bird species such as the great horned owl, plain titmouse, and water ouzel.

People float easily on the Great Salt Lake because of its high salt concentration. It is the second saltiest lake next to the Dead Sea.

Common birds include goldfinches, finches, wrens, kingfishers, swallows, sparrows, barn owls, robins, plovers, ravens, crows, magpies, hummingbirds, blackbirds, hawks, condors, quail, terns, and woodpeckers. Far less common—though still present—are golden eagles, great white pelicans, and even sea gulls (the state bird) visiting from the Pacific coast of California.

Common trees and shrubs in Utah include pine, juniper, aspen, cottonwood, maple, hawthorn, chokecherry, the Utah oak, the Joshua tree, and the blue spruce (the state tree). Utah's distinctive wildflowers include Sweet William, Indian paintbrush, and the sego lily (the state flower).

The Utah prairie dog was reclassified from an endangered species to a threatened species by the U.S. Fish and Wildlife Service. Protection of these animals has produced a slight increase in their populations.

Human encroachment and the salinization of freshwater marshes by the floodwaters of the Great Salt Lake have threatened this flora and fauna. According to the U.S. Fish and Wildlife Service, twenty-four animals and twenty-two plants in Utah are threatened or endangered. The animals on the state's threatened or endangered list include the bald eagle, the Utah prairie dog, the whooping crane, three species of chub, two species of sucker, the southwestern willow flycatcher, and the woundfin. The plants considered to be threatened or endangered are five species of cactus, the dwarf bear-poppy, five species of milk-vetch, and the autumn buttercup.

The Colorado Plateau has some of the highest proportions of globally rare native plants in the country. Yet activities such as building roads and diverting water have hurt them. Utah receives very little rainfall. So the Colorado River, which runs through southeastern Utah, no longer reaches the sea consistently. Also, it has been used to provide water for California and cities like Phoenix, Arizona, and Las Vegas, Nevada. As a result of this diverting of the Colorado River, the river's average flow—the volume of water that flows per second—is now only one-sixth of what it was seventy years ago. This drastically reduced flow and resulting low water levels mean that four of the river's fourteen native species of fish are now endangered. To help with the problem, many dams have been built on the Colorado River and its tributaries.

Mormon settlers named the Joshua tree, which thrives in Utah's deserts, after the biblical hero who led the Israelites into the Promised Land.

Chapter 2

THE HISTORY OF UTAH

At the end of the last ice age, people came to inhabit the North American continent for the first time. These Paleo-Indians, as archaeologists call them, lived in Utah from 9,000 to 5,500 BCE. They were nomadic and lived near water sources, some of which have long since disappeared. They left behind archaeological evidence, such as knife blades and fire pits, all over the state. As hunters and gatherers, they made baskets for collecting plants and stone spear tips for hunting. Mammoths, ground sloths, and other now-extinct mammals were their prey.

After 8000 BCE, the Desert Archaic people had come to replace the Paleo-Indians. In time, these people yielded to the Fremont, who appeared in northeastern Utah and the Anasazi in southern Utah. The Fremont and the Anasazi were displaced, in turn, by the Ute, Paiute, and Shoshone.

Arrival of the Europeans

After Christopher Columbus landed in the Americas in 1492, Spain quickly began colonizing the "New World." It claimed as its own the territory that stretched from the Caribbean and Mexico to Central and South America. Eventually, Spanish explorers and conquistadors reached the Pacific Coast, claiming what is today the southwestern United States and even parts of Alaska, which still bear several Spanish place names. At the time, Spain was the foremost colonial power in the world, with colonies, settlements, and outposts reaching as far as Asia. The Spanish staked a claim on all land that touched the Pacific Ocean.

In 1765, a Spanish exploration party entered the area that would become Utah. The explorers ventured no farther than the southeast corner of the present-day state. In 1776, another Spanish expedition was sent to further explore the region. Two Franciscan priests, Father Francisco Atanasio Domínguez and Father Francisco Silvestre Velez de Escalante, led the expedition. The travel journal and map of their journey attracted more Europeans to the region.

The Mormons

Mormonism originated in the early nineteenth century, a time of intense religious fervor in the frontiers of America. Many people claimed to be prophets of God. One of them, Joseph Smith Jr., founded the Church of Jesus Christ of Latter-day Saints in western New York. It is also called the Mormon Church because its sacred text is the Book of Mormon. Mormonism soon spread through missionary activity to Ohio, Missouri, and Illinois.

Two-and-a-half years after Smith's death, Brigham Young became president of the church. Church members faced persecution and violence from members of mainline Christian denominations and local governments. So Young decided to move his congregation west, outside what were then the boundaries of the United States. When he arrived in Utah, the area was still part of Mexico. Following the end of the Mexican-American War, the United States seized control of the

William Henry Jackson, an American artist who painted and photographed the American West, depicted this scene of Mormon settlers arriving in the valley that would become Salt Lake City.

entire southwest and California from Mexico. The Utah Territory became an American possession in 1848. It wasn't actually named "Utah" until 1850. The Utah Territory was named for the Ute Indians. "Ute" means "people of the mountains."

Church tradition tells of the Mormons' 1,000-mile (1,609 km) exodus from Illinois to the Salt Lake Valley in Utah. Brigham Young is said to have stopped in the valley and declared, "This is the place." He founded Salt Lake City in 1847 and became Utah's first governor.

The Long Walk

The Navajo were living in southeastern Utah and northeastern Arizona when the first European explorers and later Mormon settlers arrived in the area. Hostilities on both sides eventually culminated in the famous Long Walk. In the spring of 1864, about nine thousand Navajo men, women, and children were forced to walk more than 300 miles (483 km) to Fort Sumner in New Mexico. During the eighteen-day journey, at least two hundred Navajo died of exposure, exhaustion, dehydration, and starvation.

Those who made it to the reservation, in an area called Bosque Redondo, were forced to live in horrible conditions. The encampment was designed for half the number of people who were living there, and there was a shortage of water and firewood. The Navajo suffered from annual crop failures, caused by both man and nature. Hostile Comanches frequently raided the reservation, causing further deprivation.

In 1868, the reservation at Fort Sumner was declared a failure. That same year, the Treaty of Bosque Redondo established a new reservation for the Navajo that lay partly inside their traditional homeland, within the four sacred mountains. The treaty also provided protection for Navajo rights.

Utah's Black Hawk War

Tensions between native populations and the new arrivals soon sparked a Native American uprising against the Mormons. A young Ute warrior named Black Hawk led members of the Ute, Paiute, and Navajo tribes in raids against the Mormon settlers in central and

Mormon Practices

Joseph Smith Jr., founder of the Church of Jesus Christ of Latter-day Saints, taught that polygamy (multiple marriages) was a commandment. He wanted to follow the model of the patriarchs of the Old Testament, such as Abraham and Jacob, who were polygamists. Smith taught that one's status in the next life was based on how many wives and children one had in this life.

Smith is believed to have had thirty-three wives during his lifetime. Brigham Young, president of the Mormon Church in the mid-nineteenth century, had fifty-six wives. He had fifty-six children with nineteen of them. Back then, Mormons called the practice "celestial" or "patriarchal" marriage.

The practice of polygamy sparked outrage among many non-Mormon Americans, who viewed it as immoral. The U.S. Congress stepped in to end polygamy by passing the Morrill Anti-Bigamy Act of 1862. Bigamy is being married to more than one person at a time. President Abraham Lincoln signed it into law. However, most Mormons ignored it. Then in 1882, Congress passed the Edmunds Anti-Polygamy Act, making polygamy a felony. Many prominent polygamists, including the presiding Mormon Church president John Taylor, went into hiding.

As long as polygamy was in practice, the Utah Territory would never be allowed to become a state. For this reason, the Mormon Church banned polygamy in 1890, and an anti-polygamy clause was written into the Utah Constitution as a condition for statehood. In 1896, Utah was admitted into the Union, becoming the forty-fifth state. By 1910, the Mormon Church excommunicated (kicked out) any members still practicing polygamy.

Today, the vast majority of Mormons do not practice polygamy, but they do not say that the past practice of polygamy was wrong, either. Some fundamentalist splinter groups from the Mormon Church still practice polygamy illegally. Many of these practicing polygamists believe the church was wrong to forsake what had been a cherished doctrine. There are believed to be tens of thousands of practicing polygamists in Utah today.

southern Utah. The Mormons fought back. Both sides blamed the other for what was thereafter called the Black Hawk War (1865–1872), the longest and most deadly conflict between white settlers and Native Americans in Utah history.

Mormons attribute the cause of the war to an incident at Manti, Utah, during which local Utes and Mormons got into an argument, exchanged threats, and ended up in a fistfight. The Native Americans believed this was just one incident of many that showed the Mormons' contempt and disrespect for them.

A major source of tension between the Mormon settlers and the Native Americans was the lack of resources in Utah's harsh environment. There was a continual struggle for control over scarce food and water supplies. Food was especially hard to come by in 1864, which was a drought year. The U.S. government failed to provide enough food to the Ute reservation, and many were dying of starvation. Black Hawk himself was motivated by bitterness and revenge because his wives and children had died from measles and other diseases associated with the white settlers.

New Immigration

Until the construction of the transcontinental railway, Utah's largest immigrant group was the Mormons, who were mostly of Yankee (New England), British, or Scandinavian origin. Once the transcontinental railway was up and running, more non-Mormon immigrants began arriving from around the world. The railway attracted people looking for work, especially in the emerging mining industry. Mining for metals, coal, and minerals became extremely important to the state's economic development. English, Irish, and Welsh immigrants came to Utah to work in the mines. There was also an influx of

Shaking hands at the golden spike ceremony on May 10, 1869, were the chief engineers of the Union Pacific and Central Pacific railroads, which were joined at Promontory, Utah, to complete the transcontinental railroad.

Germans, Dutch, and Swiss immigrants. Labor recruiters brought in Italian laborers, mostly from northern Italy.

Although there were other ethnicities represented, including Chinese and African Americans, Utah continued to be predominantly white. Some fourteen thousand Chinese performed backbreaking labor on the transcontinental railroad from Sacramento, California, to Promontory, Utah. In the 1880s, a wave of anti-Chinese discrimination led to immigration restrictions. Nevertheless, the town of Ogden featured a Chinatown with more than one hundred Chinese residents. African Americans who migrated to Utah often found work as train porters or laborers. They were not welcomed into white society, so they established their own churches, newspapers, businesses, and clubs.

The European migration to Utah included Jews. Some of them converted to Mormonism. They were escaping anti-Semitism in Russia and Poland. In the 1890s, immigrants from eastern and southern Europe—Slavs, Greeks, Serbs, and Croats—came to Utah as well. The Italians and Irish, who were Catholic, tended not to mix with the Greeks and Serbs, who belonged to the Eastern Orthodox Christian churches. Utah's Hispanic population grew between 1910 and 1930, mainly due to immigration from Mexico, as well as Colorado and New Mexico. They settled in the towns of southeast Utah and found work as sheepherders, wranglers, and cattle drivers.

The Great Depression in Utah

Utah was among the states that were hardest hit by the Great Depression, which began in 1929 and lasted through the late 1930s. As was the case nationwide, unemployment rates plummeted, wages declined, banks failed, and many people lost their businesses, homes, and land. Long lines of hungry people formed outside soup kitchens. Many families that had lost their homes joined the peddlers, who sold whatever they could, on the streets. In 1933, the *Deseret News* reported that hundreds of families were camped out in vacant lots around Salt Lake City.

Utah's farmers were also hit hard. After World War I, demand for their produce fell, and the prices they received for their crops dropped sharply. At the same time, they had to deal with natural disasters such as alternating floods and drought. People found themselves in an absolutely hopeless, desperate, and humiliating situation that they could not change no matter how hard they tried.

Some people became angry at the state government's seeming inaction in the face of this economic and social catastrophe. They decided to protest. In Salt Lake City, thousands of unemployed people marched to the state capitol building carrying signs that read, "We Want Work, Not Charity" and "We Want Milk for Our Children." They demanded a halt to home foreclosures so that people who could not pay their mortgage would not be evicted from their homes. They also demanded unemployment compensation, a free school lunch program, and more. Places like Salt Lake City set up relief committees to meet some of these demands. Ultimately, however, Utah and the rest of the country had to turn to the federal government for assistance.

President Franklin D. Roosevelt's New Deal had a big impact on Utah. The Works Progress Administration (WPA), the largest New Deal agency, employed seventeen thousand Utah residents at its peak.

Utah Today

Utah is experiencing phenomenal growth, with many people migrating there each year from around the country and the world. The state economy is relatively strong, and many of the new arrivals are drawn there by jobs.

Traditionally one of the least diverse states in the nation, Utah is seeing big changes, thanks to immigration. In 1970, the state was 98 percent white, but now minorities make up 17.8 percent of the population. Hispanics, whose numbers declined during the Great Depression, are now the fastest-growing ethnic group in the state, especially in the cities. Twenty-two percent of Salt Lake City's population is Hispanic. Almost a third of West Valley City's and Ogden's populations are Hispanic. West Valley City is almost 50 percent minority or nonwhite, and other Utah cities are growing and changing in a similar fashion. In fact, the state may be even more diverse than the numbers show, since Iraqi, Serbian, Bosnian, Polish, and Greek immigrants fall statistically into the white population. A better reflection of this mini-melting pot might be a recent Utah school study showing that 117 different languages were spoken in the homes of the state's public school students.

Roast pigs and fresh fruit fill tables during a Tongan celebration in Salt Lake City. Tongan immigration to Utah began in the 1970s.

Although Utah has its share of anti-immigrant groups, most state residents feel that diversity is a benefit to the state. For example, the West Valley City Council built a Cultural Celebration Center where citizens can gather and stage cultural events. Other similar efforts are being made statewide to make new arrivals and minorities feel safe, welcome, respected, and valued in Utah.

THE GOVERNMENT OF UTAH

Like that of most U.S. states, Utah's government is divided into three branches: executive, legislative, and judicial. The state is divided into political jurisdictions known as counties. There are twenty-nine counties in Utah ranging in size from 611 square miles (1,582 sq km; Morgan County) to 7,933 square miles (20,546 sq km; San Juan County). The largest county in terms of population is Salt Lake County (1,022,651 people), while the smallest is Daggett County (only 938 people).

The Executive Branch

The governor is the head of Utah's executive branch. He or she is elected to a four-year term. The governor supervises the various offices and departments within the executive branch. These include the departments of agriculture, corrections, commerce, community and culture, environment, financial institutions, economic development, health, human services, labor, insurance, taxes, technology services, transportation, workforce services, and veterans affairs.

The Legislative Branch

The state legislature consists of a senate and a house of representatives. Senators serve four-year terms, while representatives serve

The Utah State Capitol in Salt Lake City replaced the state-house in Fillmore, Utah's first capital. The seagull, which is the state bird, is painted flying among the clouds on the inside of the dome.

two-year terms. The legislature meets each year in January for a forty-five-day session. Historically, a large majority—sometimes up to 80 percent or more—of Utah's state senators and representatives have been Mormon. (Mormons make up just over 60 percent of the state's population.) Two senators and three representatives represent the state in Congress.

Officially, the Church of Latter-day Saints stays out of politics. It only participates in political debates and attempts to sway policy

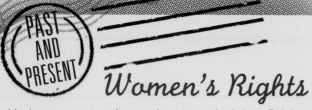

Women's Rights

Utah was once a pioneer in women's rights. Brigham Young and others wanted to act to prevent the passing of anti-polygamy legislation. They felt that if women in Utah had the right to vote, it would change the rest of the country's image of Utah women as being oppressed. So in 1870, twenty-six years before becoming a state, the territorial government granted suffrage to women. Only Wyoming granted voting rights to women earlier. Brigham Young's niece Sarah Young became the first woman voter in a municipal election.

However, in 1872, Congress passed the Edmunds Tucker Act to limit Mormon influence in Utah's government. The act was aimed primarily at polygamists, stating that they were ineligible to vote, serve on juries, or hold public office. But one of the provisions of the act also repealed the right of women to vote.

It would take a huge organized effort to win back the vote for Utah women. Women's suffrage groups formed in nineteen of Utah's twenty-seven counties. There were long debates about women's suffrage at an 1895 constitutional convention in Utah, held in preparation for statehood the following year. Ultimately, the suffrage movement succeeded, and women's right to vote was written into the new state constitution. Following the signing of its constitution, Utah became only the second state in the country (behind Colorado) to elect a woman to the state legislature in 1896. (Utah voters actually elected three women to the state House of Representatives and Senate that year.)

Today, Utah continues its proud tradition of electing women to positions of power. In 2003, Olene S. Walker became the state's first female governor. In 2009, Utah's twenty-nine-member senate had four Democratic women (the most ever) and one Republican woman. Women chair about 4 percent of Utah's legislative committees. They also make up 22.1 percent of the 104 Utah legislators.

when "there is a moral question at issue," according to its Web site. Otherwise, "the Church does not endorse political parties or candidates." Yet its conservative influence is powerful, and Mormon legislators typically vote according to their faith and church doctrine. This is why, for example, gambling has been outlawed entirely and the sale of alcohol has been strongly restricted in the state. The

Olene S. Walker, fifteenth governor of Utah, took the oath of office on November 5, 2003. She was Utah's first female governor.

Mormon Church's influence on state government is so strong that there have been only two non-Mormon governors in Utah's history.

Despite the fact that many Americans outside of Utah have reservations about Mormon politicians and the role that Mormon doctrine may play in their policymaking, several Mormons have become prominent nationwide. Harry Reid, a Democrat from Nevada and Senate Majority Leader, is a Mormon. Other well-known Mormons include Mitt Romney, a 2008 Republican presidential candidate, and Orrin Hatch, a longtime Republican U.S. senator.

The Judicial Branch

Utah has three principal levels of courts. Trials are conducted in district and justice courts. Appeals to decisions in these trials are made in the court of appeals. The state supreme court is the so-called "court of last resort," where final appeals to court decisions are made. There are five supreme court justices who are appointed by the governor and serve ten-year terms that are renewable. These justices, along with all of the judges in Utah, are subject to retention elections. This means that voters decide whether or not to keep them in their positions. The justices elect a chief justice by majority vote to serve for four years, and an associate chief justice to serve for two years.

The supreme court usually sits and hears arguments at the Matheson Courthouse in Salt Lake City, though it occasionally meets elsewhere. Oral arguments are usually delivered to the court during the first week of every month. After lawyers for each side have presented their argument, the justices confer with each other and come to a decision. One justice is then chosen to write a formal explanation of the court's decision. If the justices have not come to a unanimous decision, another justice may write a dissenting opinion—an explanation of why he or she feels the court has arrived at a faulty decision.

Chapter 4

THE ECONOMY OF UTAH

In 2008, Utah was the fastest-growing state in the United States, according to the U.S. Census Bureau. In the first decade of the twenty-first century, at the peak of the economic cycle, Utah was adding fifty-two thousand jobs to the state economy each year. These jobs continue to be created in the state's dominant industries: tourism, transportation, information technology and research, financial services, government services, and mining of natural resources.

Tourism

Tourism is one of the most important components of Utah's economy due to year-round outdoor attractions, from mountain bike trails to top-rated ski resorts. The state boasts five spectacular national parks: Arches, Bryce Canyon, Canyonlands, Capitol Reef, and Zion, each with its own unique geologic treasures. Utah also hosts many cultural events, including the Sundance Film Festival, a major showcase of work by independent filmmakers, and the Utah Shakespearean Film Festival. Temple Square, the headquarters of the Mormon Church, draws three to five million visitors a year. Sundance alone is a powerful economic engine. Since 1994, the film festival has brought more than $550 million in economic activity to Utah. In 2009, it created about 1,960 jobs

Utah's Economy

In the early days of Mormon settlement, agriculture was essentially the only industry in Utah. Mormon farmers were determined to eke out an existence on the arid land. They hoped the extreme difficulties of farming such dry land would discourage non-Mormons from also settling the territory.

By the turn of the twentieth century, the industries that employed the most men in Utah were agriculture, transportation, and manufacturing. Women mostly worked in manufacturing and domestic service. Agriculture expanded greatly in the early twentieth century with the success of the Mormons' efforts to reclaim wasteland farms. They used extensive irrigation to bring about bumper crops in normally arid valleys. They were successful at raising cattle, sheep, chickens, and turkeys. Mining also became a huge source of new wealth. The copper mining and smelting industry grew rapidly.

Today, Utah has one of the most diversified economies of the Rocky Mountain region. Yet the agricultural industry is still the main employer in the state. Crops that can be raised successfully in the state's arid environment include hay, corn, wheat, and barley. These crops are made possible by "dry farming" techniques. Moisture conservation, drought-resistant crops, and tilling (plowing and overturning soil) all promote optimum soil conditions in dry environments. The bulk of Utah's agricultural industry, however, is devoted to the raising and slaughtering of cows, sheep, and poultry, as well as dairying.

New industries have helped the state grow even more. Trade, transportation, utilities, tourism, professional and business services, education, and health services are all leading drivers of employment in Utah. In 2007, the high-tech industry added 2,600 jobs to the state economy. The areas of growth were in computer systems design, engineering services, software, and high-tech manufacturing. Indeed, Utah was the top state in the country for "economic dynamism" for its "knowledge-based, globalized, entrepreneurial, information technology-driven, and innovation-based" economy, according to the 2007 State New Economy Index.

and generated $4 million in state tax revenue.

Agriculture

Agriculture is part of Utah's cultural history, and it continues to be important to its citizens. Mormon settlers chose farming over industry as a way of living more in keeping with biblical tradition.

The red-stone arches found in Utah's Moab region are a huge attraction for tourists.

Nevertheless, Utah cannot be described as a typical agricultural state. Its arid and mountainous areas do not provide good land for crops. The Mormons overcame these obstacles in the early twentieth century by irrigating dry desert land to great success. Today, some of the state's strongest agricultural exports include dairy products, cattle, hay, hogs, and greenhouse products.

Mining, Drilling, and Engineering

Rich in natural resources, Utah is a leading miner and producer of copper, gold, silver, lead, zinc, and molybdenum. Petroleum and natural gas are also major products extracted in Utah. Eastern Utah has vast oil shale and tar sand reserves, which may represent the future of the petroleum industry.

The science and engineering departments of Utah's major universities—Brigham Young University, the University of Utah, Utah State University, and Weber State University—provide

The salt industry was one of Utah's first enterprises and continues to be an important state industry. A small fraction of what is mined is considered good enough to use as table salt. The rest is sold to de-ice roads or to make salt licks for farm animals.

brainpower for growing high-tech firms. Novell, Iomega, and Unisys, leaders in computer hardware development, are major employers in Utah, as are the state universities.

Other Industries

Other important industries in Utah are education, government, and private health care. Because of the Mormons' healthy lifestyle practices (they do not permit smoking or drinking), Utah spends less on health care per person than neighboring states do. For this reason, the state health care industry remains financially stable, even during national economic downturns.

Chapter 5

PEOPLE FROM UTAH:
PAST AND PRESENT

Utah residents have made their mark in all areas of achievement, from the arts and entertainment to science and politics. Here are just a few notable figures.

Roseanne Barr (1952–) Born to a Jewish family in Salt Lake City, Roseanne Barr became famous in the early 1980s for her standup comedy routine. This led to her having a successful television series, *Roseanne*, in which she played a wisecracking homemaker. Barr has won an Emmy, a Golden Globe, and three American Comedy Awards.

Reva Beck Bosone (1895–1983) Reva Beck Bosone was the first woman elected to the U.S. Congress from Utah (1949–1953). Bosone taught high school from 1920 to 1927. She graduated from the University of Utah College of Law in 1930 and practiced law for six years before entering politics. She was elected a Salt Lake City judge in 1936 before being elected to Congress.

Philo Farnsworth (1906–1971) At age twenty-one, Philo Farnsworth invented the first fully electronic television. His

The first woman elected to the U.S. Congress from Utah was Reva Beck Bosone. In Congress, Bosone supported conservation projects for the western United States, as well as women's rights, Native American rights, and education.

family, which was Mormon, moved to Idaho from Utah. Their new house was powered by electricity, which sparked his interest in electronics. In his lifetime, Farnsworth invented 165 different devices. These included the amplifier, cathode ray tubes, vacuum tubes, electrical scanners, and equipment for converting an optical image into an electrical signal. Farnsworth died in Salt Lake City at the age of sixty-four. He had spent the last years of his life conducting fusion research at Brigham Young University.

Anthony Geary (1947–) Luke Spencer, Anthony Geary's character on the television daytime drama *General Hospital*, started out as a hit man. He became so popular with viewers, however, that the show's writers decided to make him into a more sympathetic character. Considered by many to be the greatest and most watched moment in the history of daytime television, Luke married the beloved character Laura (played by Genie Francis) in 1981. Geary won a Daytime Emmy Award for Outstanding Lead Actor in a Drama Series.

Robert LeRoy Parker (1866–1908) Robert LeRoy Parker is better known as Butch Cassidy. He was a legendary bank robber who organized the longest series of train and bank robberies in the history of the Old West. He was born in Beaver to Mormon parents. He was so charismatic that he never had trouble finding accomplices. His gang called themselves the Wild Bunch and included several well-known outlaws, including Harry Longabaugh, otherwise known as the Sundance Kid. Butch Cassidy is remembered fondly in folklore as the "Robin Hood of the West."

The Osmonds

The Osmonds are a successful family of performers from Ogden. The original group consisted of brothers Alan, Wayne, Merrill, and Jay, who initially performed barbershop quartet (four-part harmony) music. Later, younger brothers Donny and Jimmy and sister Marie joined their older brothers in performances.

The original group began singing in 1958. They were discovered and mentored by popular singer and entertainer Andy Williams, who booked them on his weekly NBC variety program, *The Andy Williams Show*. Viewer response was so enthusiastic after their first performance that Williams asked them back, and the Osmonds became weekly fixtures on his show from 1962 through 1969. Donny, Marie, and Jimmy gradually emerged as solo artists, raking in number-one hits like Marie's "Paper Roses" and Donny's "Puppy Love." From 1976 to 1979, the Osmond brothers produced *The Donny & Marie Show*, which was a huge television hit.

Today, the Osmond family continues to make headlines. Marie sings and records country music, has appeared on Broadway, has cohosted a talk show with Donny, and sells her own line of dolls. Donny, too, still records. He has also appeared in Broadway shows and has hosted game shows. Both have appeared on *Dancing with the Stars*, and Donny won the competition in 2009. The entire family went on a fiftieth anniversary world tour in 2007–2008. Alan's eight sons have formed a performing group known as The Osmonds–Second Generation. One of these sons, David, participated in *American Idol* and was given a pass to Hollywood, but he had to drop out due to laryngitis.

The Osmonds perform on television in 1970.

34

Chief Pocatello (1815–1884) Chief Pocatello was the leader of the Shoshone tribe when the Mormons came to Utah in the late 1840s. When the newly arrived settlers caused strife for his people—by overhunting, overgrazing, and even killing some Shoshone—Pocatello led attacks against them. After the U.S. Army became involved, he entered into peace negotiations. He agreed to relocate his tribe to a reservation in Idaho. Pocatello, Idaho, was named after him.

Robert Redford (1936–) Robert Redford is a celebrity who has worn many hats. He is an actor, director, producer, environmentalist, and philanthropist. He is also the founder of the Sundance Film Festival, which is held annually in Park City. He was born in Los Angeles, California, but makes his home in Sundance, Utah. Redford received Academy Awards for Best Director for *Ordinary People* (1981) and for Lifetime Achievement (2002).

Brent Scowcroft (1925–) Brent Scowcroft, who was U.S. National Security Advisor under presidents Gerald Ford and George H. W. Bush, was born in Ogden. He has held several other government posts. Scowcroft was a leading Republican critic of the 2003 U.S. invasion of Iraq. Among his numerous enterprises, he is the founder and president of the Forum for International Policy and president of the Scowcroft Group, an international business consulting firm.

Chief Wakara (1808–1855) Chief Wakara was leader of the Ute tribe in Utah. He was known as a great warrior and diplomat. He was talented with languages and learned to speak

Former NFL quarterback and Super Bowl MVP Steve Young, of the San Francisco 49ers, is a great-great-great-grandson of Brigham Young. He holds many career titles, including Most Rushing Touchdowns by a Quarterback.

Spanish and English, which helped him establish good working relationships with European traders. Wakara was even baptized as a Mormon. However, none of this prevented conflicts between the Utes and the Mormon settlers, including the Walker War. This war ended when Wakara and Brigham Young reached an understanding and made peace.

Steve Young (1961–) A great-great-great grandson of Brigham Young, Steve Young is a prominent member of the Mormon Church and a graduate of Brigham Young University. He was voted the NFL's Most Valuable Player in 1992 and 1994. As quarterback for the San Francisco 49ers, he helped win Super Bowl XXIX in the 1994 season and was named the game's MVP. In 2005, he was inducted into the Pro Football Hall of Fame, the first left-handed quarterback to receive the honor.

Timeline

8000–1000 BCE	The Archaic people live in the Utah region.
1000–1300 CE	The Anasazi and Fremont Indians build cliff dwellings and pit house villages.
1300	The Shoshone, Ute, Paiute, Goshute, and Navajo move into the area.
1600	The Shoshone Indians control the Utah region.
1776	The Excalante-Domínguez Expedition explores Utah on the way to California.
1821	Mexico wins independence from Spain, claiming all of the Utah Territory.
1847	Mormons, led by Brigham Young, arrive in Salt Lake Valley.
1848	The United States wins the Mexican-American War; Utah is ceded to the United States.
1850	Utah becomes a U.S. territory.
1857–1858	The Utah Mormon War is fought.
1865–1868	The Black Hawk War rages.
1869	The transcontinental railway is completed at Promontory, Utah.
1873	The U.S. Congress outlaws polygamy.
1890	The Mormon Church officially ends the practice of polygamy.
1896	Utah becomes the forty-fifth state.
1919	Zion National Park is established.
1928	Bryce Canyon National Park is established.
1965	Canyonlands National Park is opened.
1996	Utah celebrates the one hundredth anniversary of its statehood.
1999	A tornado rips through Salt Lake City, doing $100 million in damage.
2002	The Winter Olympics are held in Salt Lake City.
2009	The Gallup-Healthways Well-Being Index names Utah the highest-ranking state in the country for the happiness of its residents.

State motto:	"Industry"
State capital:	Salt Lake City
State tree:	Blue spruce
State bird:	California gull
State flower:	Sego lily
State fruit:	Cherry
Statehood date and number:	January 4, 1896; forty-fifth state
State nickname:	The Beehive State
Total area and U.S. rank:	84,904 square miles (219,900 sq km); thirteenth largest state
Population:	2,736,000
Highest elevation:	King's Peak, at 13,528 feet (4,123 m)
Lowest elevation:	Beaverdam Creek, at 2,000 feet (610 m)
Major rivers:	Colorado River, Green River, Virgin River, Kanab Creek, Paria River, San Juan River, Escalante River, Dirty Devil River, Kane Springs Creek, Dolores River

State flag

State seal

Major lakes:	Great Salt Lake, Lake Powell, Utah Lake, Bear Lake, Fish Lake
Highest recorded temperature:	117°F (47°C), at St. George, July 5, 1985
Lowest recorded temperature:	-69°F (-56°C), at Peter's Sink, February 1, 1985
Origin of state name:	Named after the Ute tribe; "Ute" means "people of the moutains"
Chief agricultural products:	Cattle, dairy products, hay, turkeys
Major industries:	Machinery, aerospace, mining, food processing, electric equipment, tourism

California gull

Sego lily

GLOSSARY

anti-Semitism Prejudice against Jewish people.

arid Lacking rainfall or water.

clause A separate section of a legal document.

congregation An assembly of people, usually members of a particular church.

denomination A religious group having its own distinct beliefs.

doctrine A system of beliefs accepted by a group.

endangered To be in immediate danger of becoming extinct.

ethnic Denoting traits exhibited by a group of people with a common ancestry or culture.

excommunicated To be cut off by a church or religious community and forbidden to attend worship services or participate in any rituals of the faith.

exodus A journey by a large group escaping from a hostile environment.

legislation Laws that are enacted by a legislative body, such as Congress.

legislator Someone who makes laws by proposing, crafting, and voting for them.

migration The movement of people from one country or locality to another.

nomadic Traveling from place to place.

persecution The suffering inflicted on a person or people, especially on the basis of their race or religion.

polygamist Someone who is married to two or more people at the same time.

reservation A tract of land set apart by the government for a special purpose, especially for the use of Native American peoples.

semi-arid Describing an area that receives a low amount of precipitation, usually somewhere between 10 and 20 inches (25 and 50 cm).

settlement The establishment of colonies; a community of people smaller than a town.

threatened Describing flora or fauna that may become endangered in the near future.

tributary A branch of a river that flows into the main stream.

unanimous Being in complete agreement.

wrangler Someone employed to handle animals professionally, especially horses; a cowboy.

Brigham Young University's Museum of Peoples and Cultures

105 Allen Hall

Provo, UT 84602-3600

(801) 422-0020

Web site: http://mpc.byu.edu

The Museum of Peoples and Cultures exists to serve the academic mission of BYU and care for the anthropological, archaeological, and ethnographic collections in the custody of the university.

Bryce Canyon National Park

P.O. Box 640201

Bryce Canyon, UT 84764-0201

(435) 834-5322

Web site: http://www.nps.gov/brca/index.htm

Named after Mormon pioneer Ebenezer Bryce, Bryce Canyon became a national park in 1928. It's famous for its unique geology, consisting of a series of horseshoe-shaped amphitheaters carved from the eastern edge of the Paunsaugunt Plateau in southern Utah.

Salt Lake Convention & Visitors Bureau

90 South West Temple

Salt Lake City, UT 84101

(801) 534-4900

Web site: http://www.visitsaltlake.com/visit

The Salt Lake Convention & Visitors Bureau is a private, nonprofit community organization promoting Salt Lake as a travel destination. Each year, more than one million people utilize its visitor information centers and Web site.

Utah Division of Wildlife Resources

P.O. Box 146301

Salt Lake City, UT 84114-6301

(801) 538-4700

Web site: http://wildlife.utah.gov

This governmental organization's mission is to serve the people of Utah as the guardian of the state's wildlife.

Utah Geological Survey

1594 West North Temple

P.O. Box 146100

Salt Lake City, UT 84114

(801) 537-3300

Web site: http://geology.utah.gov

The Utah Geological Survey, a division of the Utah Department of Natural Resources, provides timely scientific information about Utah's geologic environment, resources, and hazards.

Utah Office of Tourism

Council Hall/Capitol Hill

300 North State Street

Salt Lake City, UT 84114

(801) 538-1900

Web site: http://travel.utah.gov

The Utah Office of Tourism, an office within the Governor's Office of Economic Development, works "to improve the quality of life of Utah citizens through revenue and tax relief, by increasing the quality and quantity of tourism visits and spending."

Utah State History

300 South Rio Grande Street

Salt Lake City, UT 84101

(801) 533-3500

Web site: http://history.utah.gov

This state agency within the Utah Department of Community and Culture is dedicated to providing information about Utah's history to students and teachers.

Web Sites

Due to the changing nature of Internet links, Rosen Publishing has developed an online list of Web sites related to the subject of this book. This site is updated regularly. Please use this link to access the list:

http://www.rosenlinks.com/uspp/utpp

Brown, Jonatha A. *Utah* (Portraits of the States). Strongsville, OH: Gareth Stevens Publishing, 2006.

Buff, Mary, and Conrad Buff. *Peter's Pinto: A Story of Utah*. Whitefish, MT: Kessinger Publishing, LLC, 2007.

Duncan, Dayton, and Ken Burns. *The National Parks: America's Best Idea*. New York, NY: Alfred A. Knopf, 2009.

Fine, Jil. *The Transcontinental Railroad: Tracks Across America*. New York, NY: Children's Press, 2005.

Fodor's. *The Official Guide to America's National Parks*. 13th ed. New York, NY: Fodor's, 2009.

Gunderson, Cory Gideon. *Brigham Young: Pioneer and Prophet*. Mankato, MN: Capstone Press, 2002.

Kent, Deborah. *Utah* (America the Beautiful). New York, NY: Children's Press, 2009.

Landau, Elaine. *The Mormon Trail*. New York, NY: Children's Press, 2006.

National Geographic. *National Geographic Guide to the National Parks of the United States*. 6th ed. Des Moines, IA: National Geographic, 2009.

Neri, P. J. *Utah* (From Sea to Shining Sea). New York, NY: Children's Press, 2008.

Ollhoff, Jim. *Utah* (The United States). Edina, MN: Abdo Publishing Co., 2009.

Schulte, Mary. *Great Salt Lake* (Rookie Read-About Geography). New York, NY: Children's Press, 2006.

Stefoff, Rebecca. *Utah* (Celebrate the States). New York, NY: Benchmark Books, 2009.

Trueit, Trudi Strain. *Utah* (Rookie Read-About Geography). New York, NY: Children's Press, 2007.

BIBLIOGRAPHY

Alexander, Thomas. *Utah, the Right Place*. Layton, UT: Gibbs Smith, 2003.

Bennett, Cynthia Larsen. *Roadside History of Utah*. Missoula, MT: Mountain Press Publishing Co., 1999.

Benson, A. "Mormons Discuss Racial Inequality." *Daily Utah Chronicle*, January 15, 2003. Retrieved September 2009 (http://www.dailyutahchronicle.com/news/mormonsdiscuss-racial-inequality-1.364315).

Davidson, Lee. "Census Data: Utah Population Becoming More Diverse." *Deseret News*, October 28, 2009. Retrieved November 2009 (http://www.abc4.com/mostpopular/story/Census-data-Utah-population-becoming-more-diverse/UOfXEaNQxE6vn-SVLe5UEA.cspx).

El Nasser, Haya. "Immigrants Turn Utah into a Mini-Melting Pot." *USA Today*, September 15, 2006. Retrieved August 23, 2009 (http://www.usatoday.com/news/nation/2006-09-14-utahcover_x.htm).

Lampros, Jamie. "Utah Ranks Among the Healthiest." *Standard-Examiner*, November 22, 2009. Retrieved November 2009 (http://www.standard.net/topics/health/2009/11/22/utahranks-among-healthiest).

May, Dean L. *Utah: A People's History*. Salt Lake City, UT: University of Utah Press, 2002.

McCrae, Bill. *Utah* (Moon Handbooks). 8th ed. Berkeley, CA: Avalon Travel Publishing, 2008.

PBS. "The Mormons." WGBH/Boston, 2007. Retrieved November 2009 (http://www.pbs.org/mormons).

Peterson, Eric. *Frommer's Utah*. 7th ed. New York, NY: Frommers, 2008.

Slifer, Dennis. *Guide to Rock Art of the Utah Region*. Santa Fe, NM: Ancient City Press, Inc., 2000.

INDEX

A

agriculture, 28, 29
Anasazi, 5, 12
Arches National Park, 5, 27

B

Barr, Roseanne, 31
Black Hawk, 15, 17
Black Hawk War, 17
Bonneville, Lake, 8
Bosone, Reva Beck, 31
Bosque Redondo, Treaty of, 15
Bryce Canyon, 5, 27

C

climate, 6–7, 8
Colorado Plateau, 6, 11
Colorado River, 11

E

Europeans, arrival of in the New World,
    12–13, 15
executive branch of government, 22

F

Farnsworth, Philo, 31–33
flora and fauna, 7–11
Fremont, 5, 12

G

Geary, Anthony, 33
governor, role of, 22

Great Basin and Range, 6, 8
Great Depression, 19–20
Great Salt Lake, 5, 8, 10

H

Hatch, Orrin, 25
health care, 30

I

immigrants/immigration, 17–19, 20–21

J

judicial branch of government, 25–26

L

legislative branch of government, 22–25
Long Walk, 15

M

mining, 17, 28, 29
Mormons/Church of Jesus Christ of
    Latter-day Saints, 5, 13–14, 15–17, 19,
    23–25, 27, 28, 29, 30, 33, 35, 37

N

national parks, 5, 27
Native Americans, 5, 12, 14, 15–17, 35–37
Navajo, 15
New Deal, 20

O

Ogden, 18, 21, 34, 35
Osmond family, 34

About the Author

Jacqueline Ching has written for *Newsweek* and the *Seattle Times*. She has written numerous books on colonial American and U.S. history and civics, including *Thomas Jefferson*; *Abigail Adams: A Revolutionary Woman*; *The Assassination of Martin Luther King Jr.*; and *Women's Rights: Individual Freedom, Civic Responsibility*.

Photo Credits

Cover (top, left) Buyenlarge/Hulton Archive/Getty Images; cover (top, right) © www.istockphoto.com/Michael Madsen; cover (bottom) Toby Adamson/Axiom Photographic Agency/Getty Images; pp. 3, 6, 12, 22, 27, 31, 38 © www.istockphoto.com/John Kershner; p. 4 © GeoAtlas; p. 7 © www.istockphoto.com/Christopher Russell; p. 9 George Frey/AFP/Getty Images; p. 10 © www.istockphoto.com/James Phelps; p. 11 © www.istockphoto.com/Andrew O'Neill; p. 14 Private Collection/Peter Newark American Pictures/Bridgeman Art Library; p. 18 Andrew Joseph Russell/MPI/Getty Images; pp. 21, 25, 30 © AP Images; p. 23 © www.istockphoto.com/Caleb Harper; p. 29 © www.istockphoto.com/Ben Blankenburg; p. 32 Lisa Larsen/Time & Life Pictures/Getty Images; p. 34 Michael Ochs Archives/Getty Images; p. 36 Otto Greule/Allsport/Getty Images; p. 39 (left) Courtesy of Robesus, Inc.; p. 40 Wikipedia.

Designer: Les Kanturek; Photo Researcher: Amy Feinberg